This is a story about a little girl named Amelie, who likes to draw.

Amelie's mummy has taken her shopping, so Amelie has brought her sketch book and pencil with her.

Mummy said, "Amelie, Amelie...PLEASE just keep still, I won't be long, I just need to look through these."

While Amelie waited, she reached into her little bag and got out her pencil and drawing book. She drew circles on the page enjoying the shapes her pencil made and she waited... and waited a bit more.

Amelie is quite small, she doesn't really know much about how to draw but, sometimes, when she has her drawing pad and pencil .... something extraordinary happens.

'Scribble Scrabble,

Scribble Scrabble

Amelie loves to

Dibble, Dabble.'

First, a scruffy head and one brown ear popped up from the page, followed by a wide, open mouth with lots of teeth and a lolling pink tongue.

Then finally a white furry body with sticky out fur and, at last, four long legs and a long waggy tail.

Amelie smiled.

'Mitzee!'

She whispered quietly,
afraid that mummy
might hear her.

No sooner had she spoken than Mitzee stood up, shook her fur, then, jumped down from the page and trotted across the floor of the shop.

Amelie followed, trying both to keep up with Mitzee and avoid bumping into legs and shopping bags as she ran.

At the top of the escalator, Mitzee stopped.

It gave Amelie a chance to catch her up.

"It's o.k. Mitzee, you just have to hold on to the handrail and step carefully onto the middle of a step."

Mitzee looked at Amelie, then, with a huge leap, landed half way down the escalator.

Amelie followed, holding the handrail tightly.

Smelling the fresh air from the open door Mitzee bounded out, her long legs carrying her along very fast.

Amelie rushed out behind her scribble dog. Luckily, Mitzee had followed the path by the river and not the path to the car park where she could get run over.

At the water's edge, Mitzee startled a jogger which slowed her down. Amelie again caught up with Mitzee. Holding on to the dog's pink collar, they walked along together until ...

Amelie wasn't sure how ... Mitzee leaped into the air, startling a group of swans who hissed angrily at her.

"HISS HISS."

Rushing in between their wings, and beaks, getting pecked at as she went, Mitzee got muddier and wetter and more excited by the moment.

Amelie knew that swans were strong and could hurt a child, or a dog, with their wings so she tried to calmly call Mitzee back...

Mitzee was having too much fun to listen and had now moved on to where some ducks were at the river edge. She loved to watch them fly into the air as she ran, hearing them quack angrily at her. QUACK QUACK!

Coming to a sliding stop, Amelie slipped on the wet mud, before managing to grab Mitzee's collar and calm her down.

'Naughty girl' Amelie said crossly 'you could have hurt those poor birds.'

She walked her purposefully back to the double doors and into the shop...

"Amelie! How on earth have you got so dirty just standing there? Look at your muddy jeans!"

Amelie thought mummy was cross.

"Sorry." said Amelie as she slipped her drawing book back into her little bag, just catching sight of Mitzee's long wet tail as it slid back into the page.